My VP Looks Like Me

by Dr. Phyllis Harris

Illustrated by Elsa Achu

To Tori
Hello Beautiful ♡
Your mom thinks you are smart and wanted you to have this book. I hope you enjoy my book as much as I enjoyed writing it. Continue to be the best you Princess
Love,
Dr. Phyllis Harris

This is a work of fiction. Names, characters, places, and incidents either are the product of the author's imagination or are used fictitiously. Any resemblance to actual persons, living or dead, events, or locales is entirely coincidental.

Copyright © 2021 by Dr. Phyllis Harris

All rights reserved. No part of this book may be reproduced or used in any manner without written permission of the copyright owner except for the use of quotations in a book review.

First hardback edition June 2021

Book illustrations by Elsa Achu

ISBN: 978-1-09838-246-9 (hardback)

Dedication

I would like to dedicate this book to my family and loved ones, especially my children Andre Jr. (Devyn), Ryan (Dorothy), and Ariel. Your independence and drive for success is truly amazing. May you one day be the VP that someone sees when they look in the mirror.

I am always fascinated by my grand kids; Doreun, Makaila, Zion, Rylee, Rylyn, Aaliyah, Nia, Nyla and Akai. They are the therapy for my well-being. I love each and everyone of you and I pray that this book will inspire you to be the best at everything you do.

In loving memory of our Yorkshire Terrier, Chase

TODAY AT SCHOOL, WE TALKED ABOUT CAREER CHOICES.

WE LEARNED THAT A CAREER IS A JOB JOURNEY THAT REQUIRES SPECIAL SKILLS, TRAINING, AND LEARNING FOR LIFELONG WORK.

OUR TEACHER TOLD US TO GO HOME AND THINK ABOUT CAREER CHOICES, AND WHAT WE WOULD LIKE TO BE WHEN WE GROW UP.

EXCITED ABOUT THE HOMEWORK ASSIGNMENT . . .
WHEN I GOT OFF THE BUS, I RAN IN THE HOUSE
YELLING, "**MOM, MOM**" SHE REPLIED, "YES, DEAR?"
THEN I SAID, "I NEED A JOB, I NEED A CAREER!"

I TOLD HER ABOUT OUR CAREER-DAY LESSON AND WHAT I NEEDED TO DO, AND SHE LOOKED AT ME AND SAID, "BABY GIRL, YOU CAN BE WHATEVER YOU WANT; I SEE A VP OR PRESIDENT IN YOU!"

SHE SMILED PROUDLY AS I WALKED TOWARD MY ROOM.

WHILE PLAYING WITH MY DOLLS AND TEACHING THEM THEIR ABCS,

I THOUGHT TO MYSELF, '*HMM, A TEACHER IS WHAT I MIGHT WANT TO BE.*'

I COULD TEACH HOW TO COUNT, WRITE, SPELL, AND MAYBE A LITTLE ABOUT HISTORY.

BUT FIRST, I MUST MAKE SURE A TEACHER LOOKS GOOD ON ME.

SO, I CHECK MY MIRROR, AND I SAY TO MYSELF, "IF I BECOME A TEACHER, I'LL BE THE BEST TEACHER THAT I CAN BE."

THEN ALL OF A SUDDEN, I LOOK CLOSELY AT MY MIRROR IMAGE, AND ALL I CAN SEE IS THAT MY VP LOOKS LIKE ME.

"TIME TO WALK YOUR DOG!" MY MOM YELLS.

MY DOG DEPENDS ON ME, AND I LOVE TAKING GOOD CARE OF HIM. MAYBE, JUST MAYBE, I SHOULD BE A VETERINARIAN.

WHEN AT THE ZOO, I FEED THE ANIMALS, I TALK TO THEM, AND I PET THEM TOO.

A VETERINARIAN JUST MIGHT LOOK GOOD ON ME.

SO, I CHECK MY MIRROR AND I SAY TO MYSELF, "IF I BECOME A VETERINARIAN, I'LL BE THE BEST VETERINARIAN THAT I CAN BE."

THEN ALL OF A SUDDEN, I LOOK CLOSELY AT MY MIRROR IMAGE, AND ALL I CAN SEE IS THAT MY VP LOOKS LIKE ME.

IT'S KARAOKE NIGHT, AND I LOVE TO SING.

I SING WHEN I'M HAPPY, I SING ALL DAY; I SING MYSELF TO SLEEP AND DREAM OF SINGING IN A SCHOOL PLAY.

"A SINGER! THAT'S IT; THAT'S WHAT I'LL BE. I'M SURE A SINGER LOOKS GOOD ON ME."

SO I CHECK MY MIRROR AND I SAY TO MYSELF, "IF I BECOME A SINGER, I'LL BE THE BEST SINGER THAT I CAN BE."

THEN, ALL OF A SUDDEN, I LOOK CLOSELY AT MY MIRROR IMAGE, AND ALL I CAN SEE IS THAT MY VP LOOKS LIKE ME.

HELPING MY MOM COOK DINNER IS ALWAYS FUN.

WHEN IN THE KITCHEN, THERE'S LOTS OF EXPERIMENTS AND INVENTIONS. INSTEAD OF A CHEF ON MY CAREER LIST, I FEEL MORE LIKE A SCIENTIST.

A SCIENTIST? YES INDEED, A SCIENTIST WOULD LOOK GOOD ON ME.

SO I CHECK MY MIRROR, AND I SAY TO MYSELF, "IF I BECOME A SCIENTIST, I'LL BE THE BEST SCIENTIST THAT I CAN BE."

THEN ALL OF A SUDDEN, I LOOK CLOSELY AT MY MIRROR IMAGE, AND ALL I CAN SEE IS THAT MY VP LOOKS LIKE ME.

ALL THIS TALK ABOUT BECOMING A SCIENTIST HAS GOT ME READY TO EXPLORE; I'M FEELING GUTSY AND THINKING OF BEING AN ASTRONAUT AND A WHOLE LOT MORE.

TO LAUNCH INTO SPACE WOULD BE A DREAM COME TRUE. MANY WOMEN HAVE DONE IT BEFORE, AND I CAN DO IT TOO. AN ASTRONAUT? HMM, YES, I CAN SEE AN ASTRONAUT WOULD REALLY LOOK GOOD ON ME.

SO, I CHECK MY MIRROR AND I SAY TO MYSELF, "IF I BECOME AN ASTRONAUT, I'LL BE THE BEST ASTRONAUT THAT I CAN BE."

THEN ALL OF A SUDDEN, I LOOK CLOSELY AT MY MIRROR IMAGE, AND ALL I CAN SEE IS THAT MY VP LOOKS LIKE ME.

"WHAT'S THE MATTER, DEAR, ARE YOU HAVING TROUBLE DECIDING ON A CAREER?" I LOOKED AT MY MOM AND SAID, "I'M STILL NOT SURE OF WHAT I WANT TO BE," AND SHE REPLIED, "I THOUGHT YOU WANTED TO BE A JUDGE, JUST LIKE ME?"

BEING A JUDGE WOULD BE FUN AND REWARDING. AS A JUDGE, I COULD HELP PROTECT THE RIGHTS OF CITIZENS AND SERVE MY COMMUNITY. MAKING SOMEONE'S LIFE BETTER WOULD BE A GREAT CAREER FOR ME. I THINK A JUDGE WOULD LOOK GOOD ON ME.

SO, I CHECK MY MIRROR, AND I SAY TO MYSELF, "IF I BECOME A JUDGE, I'LL BE THE BEST JUDGE THAT I CAN BE."

THEN, ALL OF A SUDDEN, I LOOK CLOSELY AT MY MIRROR IMAGE, AND ALL I CAN SEE IS THAT MY VP LOOKS LIKE ME.

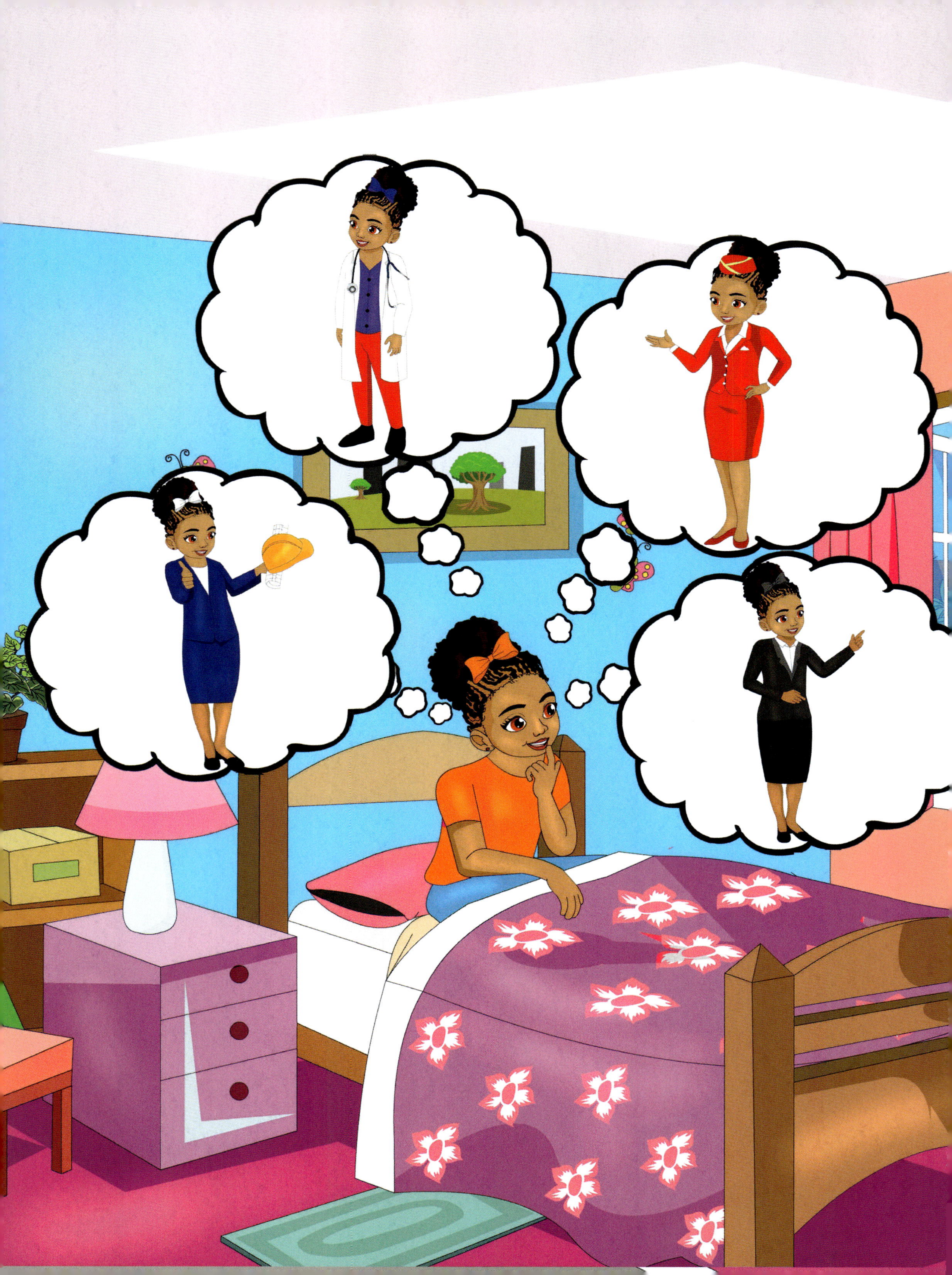

I CHECK MY MIRROR OVER AND OVER, AND I START TO BELIEVE THAT EVERY CAREER CHOICE MAKES ME FEEL HAPPY; THEY ALL LOOK GOOD ON ME.

I CAN BE A DOCTOR, AN ENGINEER, WORK IN SALES AND SERVICE, OR EVEN IN HOSPITALITY.

My VP Looks Like Me
My VP Looks Like Me
My VP Looks Like Me
My VP Looks Like Me

SO, I CHECK MY MIRROR ONE LAST TIME, AND I SAY TO MYSELF, "WHATEVER IT IS THAT I BECOME, I'LL BE THE BEST THAT I CAN BE."

THEN, ALL OF A SUDDEN, I LOOK CLOSELY AT MY MIRROR IMAGE AND MY VP SAYS TO ME,

"WHILE I MAY BE THE FIRST WOMAN IN THIS OFFICE, I WILL NOT BE THE LAST." — KAMALA HARRIS

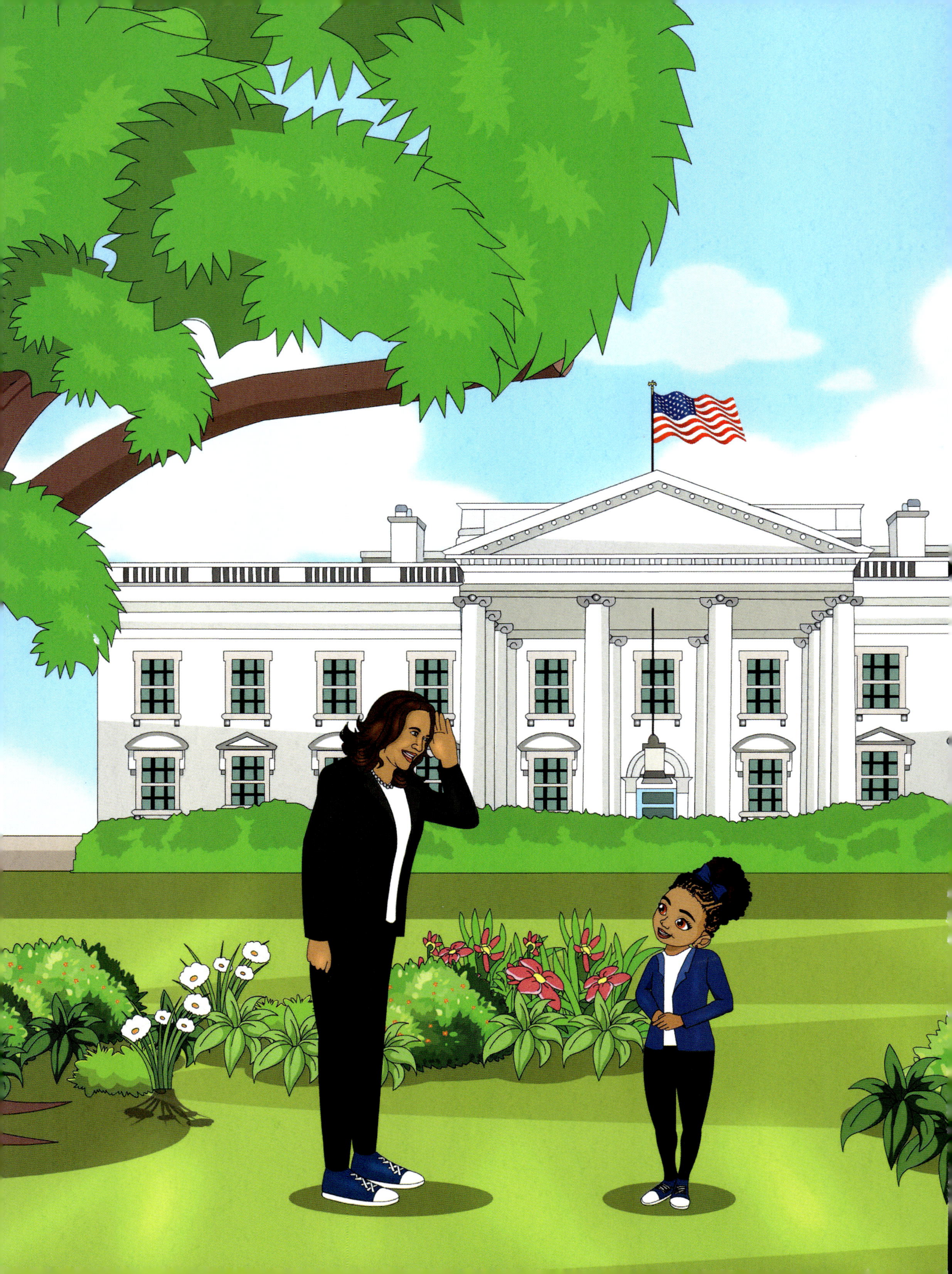

I HELD MY HEAD UP HIGH AND FELT INSPIRED TO SAY, "MADAM VP, YOU HAVE PAVED A PATH FOR FUTURE GENERATIONS TO SEE HISTORIC ACHIEVEMENTS AS ORDINARY, AND BECAUSE OF YOU . . .

I THINK A PRESIDENT LOOKS GOOD ON ME!

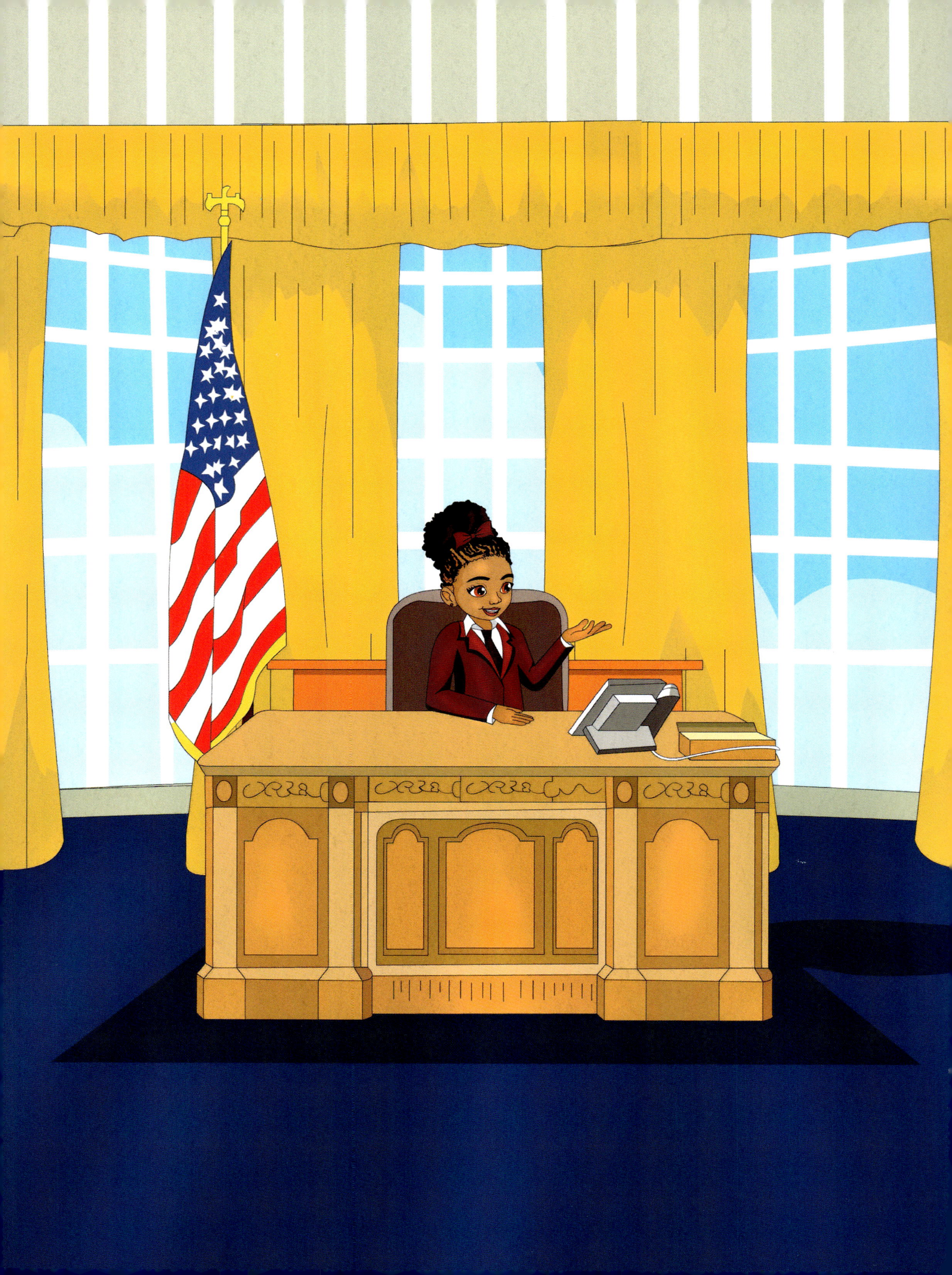

A PRESIDENT IS WHAT I'LL BE!